JERI ANN

90 EPI

26500

265-368P

Walt Disney's Mickey Mouse and the Peanuts

Written by Cindy West

Illustrated by Gene Biggs and Roy Wilson

A Golden Book • New York

Western Publishing Company, Inc., Racine, Wisconsin 53404

"Peanuts are magic,"
Mickey Mouse said to
Donald Duck.

"Come and take a walk
with me.
I will show you
what peanuts can do."

Mickey and Donald
went to see Goofy.
"I am so sad,"
said Goofy.
"I have nothing
to do."

"Here is something
to do," said Mickey.
"Put this peanut
on your nose."

Goofy put the peanut
on his nose.
He ran with the peanut
on his nose!

"Good for you!"
said Mickey.
"Good for me!"
said Goofy.
"I am happy now!"
"The peanut did it!"
said Mickey.

Mickey and Donald
went to see Minnie.
"Can you help me?"
she asked.
"My house is too quiet."

"This will help you,"
said Mickey.

He put peanuts
on the window.
"Peep! Peep! Peep!"
Birds came flying
to the window.

Bluebirds!
Redbirds!
Yellow birds, too!
"My house is not too
quiet now!" said Minnie.
"The peanuts did it!"
said Mickey.

Mickey and Donald
went to the park.
Daisy was there.

"Help! Help!"
she cried.
"My friend fell
into the water!"

"Where is your friend?"
asked Mickey.
"There she is!"
said Daisy.

"See that ladybug?"
said Daisy.
"You must save her!"

"This will save her!"
said Donald.
He took a nut
and made a boat!

"You did it!"
said Daisy.
"You saved my friend."
"The peanut did it!"
said Donald.

Pluto came by.
He barked and barked.
"Pluto wants to eat,"
said Mickey.

"It is time
to go home.
I will make
a big dinner."

Pluto barked
all the way home.
"I wish he would stop,"
said Donald.

"What is for dinner?"
asked Daisy.
"Wait and see,"
said Mickey.

"Woof! Woof! Woof!"
Pluto barked and barked.
"He will not stop,"
said Donald.

"Surprise!" said Mickey.
"Peanut butter!"
"I love peanut butter!"
said Daisy.

"I do, too!"
said Donald.
"Woof! Woof! Woof!"
barked Pluto.

They all ate.
They all ate
a lot of
peanut butter.

"Did you like
your dinner?"
asked Mickey.
"Yes!" said Donald.
"Yes!" said Daisy.
Pluto tried to bark.
He could not.
He could not
open his mouth.

"Hurray!" said Donald.
"Pluto has stopped barking!"
"The peanut butter did it!"
said Mickey.
Pluto just smiled and smiled.